TERRELL DAVIS

TERRELL DAVIS TD

Jeff Savage

LERNER SPORTS
A DIVISION OF LERNER PUBLISHING GROUP

For Bryan Bottero, football's newest star

This book is available in two editions:
Library binding by Lerner Publications Company
Soft cover by First Avenue Editions
Divisions of Lerner Publishing Group
241 First Avenue North
Minneapolis, Minnesota 55401 U.S.A.

Website address: www.lernerbooks.com

Library of Congress Cataloging-in-Publication Data

Savage, Jeff. 1961–
      Terrell Davis : TD / Jeff Savage.
           p.   cm.
      Includes bibliographical references (p.) and index.
      Summary: A biography of the Denver Broncos running back who was
chosen the Most Valuable Player in the 1998 Super Bowl.
      ISBN 0–8225–3676–5 (alk. paper)
      ISBN 0–8225–9847–7 (pbk. : alk. paper)
      1. Davis, Terrell, 1972– Juvenile literature. [1. Football
players—United States—Biography—Juvenile literature. 2. Davis,
Terrell, 1972–. 3. Football players. 4. Afro-Americans—
Biography.] I. Title.
GV939.T43S38   2000
796.332'092—dc21
      [B]   99–27304

Manufactured in the United States of America
1 2 3 4 5 6 – JR – 05 04 03 02 01 00

Contents

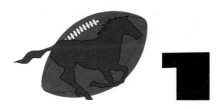

Super Bowl Hero

Crunch time. The Denver Broncos had the football deep in Green Bay territory. Everybody knew what was coming next. The 70,000 fans at Qualcomm Stadium in San Diego knew, and so did the 800 million people around the world watching the 1998 Super Bowl on television. The 11 Packers defenders braced themselves. Could they stop Terrell Davis?

The first quarter was winding down with the score tied at 7. The Packers had scored first on quarterback Brett Favre's pass to Antonio Freeman. Then Terrell had evened the score by stampeding through the defense and plowing into the end zone. He had gained 61 yards already.

Terrell took the **handoff** from John Elway and headed right. Suddenly Terrell cut left, into the teeth of the Packers defense. He lunged toward the goal line. The knee of Green Bay's Santana Dotson cracked him in the head and Eugene Robinson smacked him to the ground. *Crunch time.*

Terrell lay dizzy at the 5-yard line. The left side of his head throbbed. Sparkly lights were everywhere. He got to his knees, but he couldn't stand up. He blinked hard and shook his head, but the flashing lights popped bright as fireworks. "Just relax," teammate Shannon Sharpe told him. Broncos trainers lifted Terrell to his feet and helped him off the field.

From the sideline, Terrell squinted at the fuzzy figures on the field. "It was like a collage," he said. "Like if you've got a bunch of pictures, and you cut them up and put them on a board. A million pictures on a board." On first **down,** the Broncos ran a play for 2 yards. Terrell's head was still fuzzy, but he ran onto the field for the next play. He took the handoff from Elway and bulled headlong to the 1-yard line. *Bang!* The gun went off to end the first quarter. At the sound of it, Terrell went blind.

Waves of sickness washed over his body. "Not today, man," he said to himself. "Not today." Terrell knew what his trouble was. He was having a migraine. He had suffered from these horrible headaches since he was a young boy. "What brings them on?" he said. "I have no idea." Still, Terrell had tried everything to prevent them. He stopped drinking coffee. He had braces put on his teeth. He saw doctors regularly and took medication daily.

As the rest of the Broncos offense headed to the other end of the field to start the second quarter, Terrell went to his sideline. "I can't see," he said. "I can't see!" At once, the trainers surrounded him.

A Broncos trainer tries to help Terrell feel better.

Then his vision returned enough for him to see blurred shapes and colors. He saw coach Mike Shanahan appear before him. Then he saw another coach Shanahan, and another. He saw *three* coach Shanahans. "I can't see," he told the coach Shanahan in the middle. The coach replied that he didn't need to see. He said that the next play would be a fake to Terrell, and that Elway would run a **quarterback sneak.** Terrell had to be on the field to fool the Packers, the coach explained, for the play to work. "As long as you know I can't see," Terrell answered. "Just go over the top," said the coach.

Terrell jogged onto the field, his head pounding with every step. Elway called the play in the huddle: "Fake 15, Lead QB, Keep Pass Right, Fullback Slide." The players crouched in their stances. Terrell surged forward at the snap. Elway pinned the ball to Terrell's belly, then slyly pulled it away. The Packers focused on Terrell, just as the coach had said they would. Elway sprinted around the right end and went untouched into the end zone. A roar rang out around the stadium as Terrell got to his feet and found his quarterback in the end zone. They stood eye to eye and exchanged firm hand gestures in what had become known as the Mile High Salute.

Terrell had invented the move and had studied a Marine Corps manual to learn just how to do it.

Terrell jogged back to the Broncos' sideline a hero. "To play in pain like that," said teammate Brian Habib, "really showed his guts." Terrell's head was pounding and his stomach felt sour. A trainer greeted him with migraine nasal spray. Terrell took two sniffs in his left nostril, then two sniffs in his right nostril. Then he threw up all over his cleats. He was helped to a bench. There, doctors hooked him up with an oxygen mask and draped a white towel over his head. When the noise grew unbearable, Terrell went to the locker room.

Terrell thought he had done everything right the night before the Super Bowl. First, he had taken a warm bubble bath. Next, he had eaten his three scoops of vanilla ice cream with chocolate candies sprinkled on top. Finally, he had set the air conditioner on high, unplugged the phone, and adjusted the curtains to make the room pitch-dark. And sure enough, he had slept like a log.

On the day of the big game, he had taped his ankles, strapped on his pads in the correct order, and made sure his socks were at equal height. But Terrell had forgotten to do one thing, and he remembered it when the migraine struck. He had forgotten to take his migraine medication one hour before the game. He had not taken his migraine pill until just 10 minutes before kickoff. By then, it was too late.

Terrell is a powerful runner who relies on **cutbacks** and quickness, but his biggest strength is his vision. "I can see the hole opening as fast as anybody," he said. "I can see the big picture." But his eyes weren't helping him now. As he lay motionless in the dark training room, his teammates were struggling out on the field. Luckily, they recovered a fumble and kicked a field goal. But the high-flying Packers roared back to score on Favre's touchdown pass to Mark Chmura. The Broncos still led, 17–14, when the second quarter ended, but how long could their lead last without their best player? In the second quarter without their star, they had managed just 14 yards on offense. Their total yards rushing? Zero.

Terrell heard his teammates trudge into the locker room. He opened his eyes and sat up. He came out from the training room into the light. Players looked up from their stools at him, and coaches drawing on chalkboards turned toward him. He could see! The nasal spray had worked! "Sorry I was gone for a while there," he told everyone. "But I'm cool now."

Terrell scored three touchdowns against the Packers.

Terrell's body surged with electricity as he ran onto the field to start the third quarter. "Nineteen Toss," said Elway in the huddle. Terrell took the pitch and headed left. He felt stronger than ever, but he fumbled. The Packers recovered the ball at the 26-yard line. Moments later, they kicked a field goal to tie the score, 17–17. Terrell was angry at himself. "That won't happen again," he told his teammates.

After that, Terrell simply ran over the Packers. He went wild with bursts up the middle and swings to the outside. He led the Broncos the length of the field and smashed into the end zone to give them a 24–17 lead after three quarters.

But the Packers weren't done yet. They were the defending Super Bowl champions, and they had two-time NFL Most Valuable Player Brett Favre on their side. Plus, the Broncos had played in four other Super Bowls and had lost all four. "We have been the brunt of jokes forever," said Broncos owner Pat Bowlen. The Packers surprised no one by zipping down the field in the fourth quarter to tie the score on Favre's third touchdown pass of the day.

The sky turned dark as the clock ticked down . . . 10 minutes to go, 9 minutes, 8 minutes . . . the teams exchanged punts . . . 7 minutes, 6 minutes . . . the pace quickened . . . 5 minutes, 4 minutes . . . Denver took possession at midfield with 3 minutes and 27 seconds left. Terrell ran past a defender who yanked him down by his face mask. The penalty moved the ball to the 32-yard line. Terrell bulldozed for another yard. Then the Broncos tricked the Packers. With everyone expecting Terrell to get the ball again, Elway dumped a pass to fullback Howard Griffith who rumbled to the 8-yard line. Then Terrell blasted 7 yards to the 1. But that play was wiped out because of a penalty on Denver, and the ball was moved back to the 17-yard line. No problem. On the very next play, Terrell exploded past three defenders to the 1-yard line again.

The Packers knew stopping Terrell was impossible. He could gain yardage any time he wanted. So the Packers decided to let him score on the next play so they could get the ball back and try for the tie.

Green Bay's desperation gamble failed. When Favre's fourth-down pass was batted away, John Elway's wife turned to Terrell's mother in the stands and said, "Kateree, your son allowed our dream to come true!" In the middle of the mob scene on the field, came the announcement over the loudspeaker. Terrell had been named the Most Valuable Player of the Super Bowl. In the locker room, Terrell praised his offensive line, his fullback, his quarterback, and his coaches. "Me?" he said, shrugging. "I'm just a piece of the puzzle."

Terrell had rushed for 157 yards and three touchdowns despite missing an entire quarter with a migraine. Asked what he thought his performance meant, Terrell smiled and said, "It shows that you can never give up. A lot of people tell you what you can't do. Don't listen to them. Anything is possible. I proved that today."

Kateree and her baby boy—Terrell

A Hard Struggle

Terrell grew up just five miles from the stadium where he became a Super Bowl hero. Terrell's parents, Kateree and Joe Davis, were already raising five boys—Joe Jr., James, Reggie, Bobby, and Tyrone—when Kateree decided to move the family from St. Louis, Missouri. She loaded the boys and their belongings on a bus and headed for Southern California. Joe followed a few weeks later. "I was tired of being broke," Kateree said. "I thought the change would be good for Joe."

The family moved into a small house at 3763 Florence Street in southeast San Diego, one of the poorest and most dangerous areas of Southern

California. Joe took a job as a welder, and Kateree worked double shifts at a nursing home while she studied to be a nurse. On October 28, 1972, shortly after the move, Terrell was born. And soon after Terrell's birth, his father went to prison for six months for reckless driving. When Terrell was three, Joe Davis was sent back to prison for two years for grand theft.

Sometimes Terrell's father could be fun. Pops, as his sons called him, would race go-carts with the boys in the street, cook up big batches of food, and crack wild jokes. He would put on loud music and dance around the house with Terrell's mom. Soon, all the boys would be dancing and clapping and laughing like mad. But Pops kept getting in trouble with the law. He would get drunk and drive his car through red lights and up on curbs.

Terrell's father often beat him. He punched and kicked and lashed Terrell's bare bottom with an extension cord. Worst were those painful jabs in the chest by his father's finger. Pops jabbed his sons when he had a point to make. If Terrell failed to address an adult as "sir" or "ma'am," he was whipped. One time, a rowdy group of boys confronted Terrell and his brothers. Soon, fists were flying. Terrell ran home to get Pops to help, but instead Pops beat Terrell for leaving his brothers.

When Terrell was six years old, he started a paper route. At first, he tossed the newspapers from the backseat of his mother's car. When he was a little older, he threw them from his bicycle. As a high school student, Terrell delivered the papers from his white motor scooter.

When Terrell was seven, his family moved a mile away to a five-bedroom house on Latimer Street. But a year later, Terrell's mom and dad separated. Terrell went with three of his brothers and Pops back to Florence Street.

As a youngster, Terrell loved to build things and play sports.

Terrell loved to build things, first cars and castles with his Lego set, then model airplanes and ships with his brother Joe. Of all Terrell's brothers, Tyrone, or Terry, was his best pal. They were just a year apart and even shared the same twin bed for six years. "Terrell was a good kid," his mother said, "especially after dealing with all those knucklehead brothers."

Pops taught Terrell and his brothers how to use a knife and load and shoot a gun. Pops wanted his boys to be tough. Terrell feared his father's violent late-night rages. One time, Terrell's father pulled him and his brothers out of bed at 2 A.M. and lined them up against a wall. Pops raised a gun and ordered them not to move. He fired one bullet over each of their heads. He wanted to see how brave they were. None of the boys moved. Another time, Pops fired a gun at a neighbor, who fired back. Other neighbors called the police, who took Terrell's father away.

Terrell had another childhood struggle. He was seven when he got his first migraine. He had no idea what was happening to him. He was sitting against a fence in a parking lot, waiting for his mother to pick him up from football practice, when his vision suddenly went blurry. "I was like, 'Man, I'm going blind,'" he said. "I would look at things and all I would see were these big blotches. I got scared and started to panic. I'm whining like, 'Where's my mom at?' I'm thinking, 'Is this how it happens for blind people?'" When Kateree finally arrived, Terrell climbed into her car, and his vision started to clear. As it did, though, a dull throbbing began in his head. By the time they reached home, his head was pounding. His mother gave him soup and aspirin and put him to bed. That did not help. Terrell cried himself to sleep but woke up at midnight and threw up on the bedroom floor. He cleaned himself up and went back to bed.

Terrell did not suffer another migraine until he was 13, but then the headaches started coming every few weeks. They would strike at any time—in math class, at the bowling alley, on the football field. Flashing lights or even a complete loss of vision would be the warning sign, and then his head would be filled with pain. He learned that lying down in a dark, quiet, cool room helped. But the misery still lasted for hours, and he would almost always vomit. "My biggest worry was not having a name for it, not knowing what it was," Terrell said. "I'd always leave the house with the fear that, this is the day it could come."

One time, when Terrell could not read the chalk-board, the teacher sent him to the office. The principal called Pops to come and get him. At home, Terrell couldn't even hang up his jacket in the closet. Pops yelled at him. "I kept trying, but I couldn't do it," Terrell said. "My depth perception and motor skills were off." Pops tore his belt from his pants, yanked down Terrell's pants, and gave him a fierce whipping.

One thing Terrell could count on from his father was fan support. Pops never missed a Pop Warner Football game. And he always yelled and cheered louder than anyone else. Terrell played his games on a dirt field at Valencia Elementary School. Pops sat with about 40 other people on the crickety wooden bleachers. Terrell's first team, when he was seven, was the Buccaneers. He played offensive right guard, and his brother Terry played left guard. Together the Davis boys flattened their opponents so hard they often cried.

The next season, coach Frank White switched Terrell to running back. Terrell was no bigger than the other players, but he bowled them over. He just ran straight ahead. Some games, he gained 200 yards, others 300. One game, he ran for more than 400. His nickname was Boss Hogg.

Frank White coached Terrell in youth football.

"Terrell was a legend," said coach White. "He had a reputation throughout the county. Everybody would want to know who this Boss Hogg character is." Opponents knew who was going to carry the ball and would shout, "Look out for number 30!" So coach White would put Terrell in jersey number 31 at halftime. The trick would work for a minute or so in the third quarter until he broke another long run. The next game, he would wear number 32 and switch to number 33 at halftime.

"Everybody knew the ball was going to him," coach White said, "but nobody wanted to be in the hole when he got there because when he hit that hole he hit it so fast—boom! He didn't lift any weights, but he was nothing but a muscle. He not only listened to you, he heard you. Whenever you asked him to do something, all you ever heard was 'Yes, sir,' 'No, sir,' 'Yes, coach,' 'No, coach.'"

Terrell was 10 when Mom and Pops got back together. They all moved back into the big house on Latimer Street, and Pops settled down a bit. He bought the boys skateboards and remote-controlled cars. Pops also often led his sons on long daytime walks to downtown San Diego, the boys eating french fries and candy all the way.

At Bell Junior High School, Terrell played all sports, though football was clearly his best game. In basketball, he struggled with his dribbling skills. In baseball, he struck out more often than he thought he should.

Terrell was playing baseball at Martin Luther King Park with three of his brothers one day when a family friend came to pick up the boys. Pops had been sick and the woman was coming to drive them to the hospital. Seeing her speed down the street, Terrell got a spooky feeling. When the boys reached the hospital, they saw their sobbing mother. Pops had died. A disease, called **lupus,** had invaded his body, and his heart had given out.

"I still remember looking at Pops the day he died," said Terrell. "I remember thinking, 'Blink an eye, get up, say something, say you're playing.' I'm looking at him like, 'This can't be it.'"

Terrell's father—Joe Davis

They buried Pops a week later, on the day he would have been 42 years old. Terrell did not leave his room for three weeks. Most days, he slept until noon. He stopped doing his homework. His grades went from A's and B's to F's. The other boys took their dad's death even harder. Terry pushed a teacher to the ground and had to spend 245 days at a juvenile work camp. Bobby shot a pregnant woman in a robbery. The woman survived, but the baby did not. Bobby served six years in prison.

Terrell attended Morse High School but did not pay attention in class. He flunked all his classes. He even failed physical education because he did not try. Terrell did not go out for the football team as a freshman or sophomore. "When Pops died, all life just came out of me," he said. "The struggle was a long, hard one for me."

Terrell and his brothers struggled after their dad died.

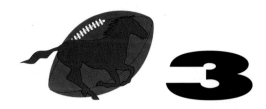

Finding His Way

One day, in the middle of his sophomore year of high school, Terrell had a change of heart. He realized that his failing grades had put him on a fast track to disaster. "I watched my brothers do things that changed their lives for the worse," he said, "and I couldn't let that happen to me."

Terrell decided to take charge of his life. He started helping his mom around the house. Kateree Davis was always taking in people who needed help. Terrell's grandfather was ill and living with them. Terrell bathed him every night. Family friends who were too poor to live anywhere else lived in the Davis home. Terrell helped with their meals and laundry. One time, Terrell counted as many as 12 people living in his house. His favorite housemate was Jamaul Pennington, his best friend.

Terrell decided he wanted to go to college, so he started paying attention in class and doing his homework. But he couldn't seem to shake his reputation as a poor student at Morse. His mother encouraged him to transfer to nearby Lincoln High School. Jamaul went to Lincoln. The two friends became study buddies, as well. They challenged each other on homework and tests. Soon, A's and B's appeared on Terrell's report cards again. He even went to summer school to make up for lost time at Morse.

In the spring, Terrell joined the track team. He hadn't lost his speed and power, and he set school records in the 400-meter dash and the discus throw. Before Terrell's junior year started, his old coach, Frank White, told him: "Boss, you need to go back to playing football. You're wasting your talent by sitting around and not playing." Terrell agreed. Marcus Allen had played football for Lincoln and earned a scholarship to the University of Southern California, where he won the Heisman Trophy as the nation's best college player. Terrell thought maybe he could be the next Marcus Allen at Lincoln.

Terrell wanted to play running back, but other boys had earned those positions. The only way Terrell could get in the games was to play on the line. So he volunteered to be a **nose tackle.** He led the Hornets in tackles and sacks. Coach Tony Jackson said, "Blocking him was like trying to block a greased pig." Terrell missed being Boss Hogg, but he was happy to be playing again.

Terrell and Jamaul shared their plans for their future. Jamaul wanted to join the Navy, and Terrell wanted to go to college and study accounting. Someday, the two wanted to open a dance club together. In the meantime, they played ball in the street, or studied at the library or in Terrell's room. Whenever Terrell got a crippling migraine, Jamaul would fix him some tea, shut off the light, and tell everyone in the house to quiet down. "He didn't know what was wrong with me," said Terrell. "He just knew that I would get sick sometimes and he would have to take care of me."

One time, Jamaul wasn't there to help. Terrell was in Washington, D.C., with his football team. The Hornets had just scrimmaged another high school and were out sightseeing when Terrell's migraine struck. The noise and shouting of 60 boys filled the bus as it rolled past the White House and Washington Monument and other famous sites. Terrell sat slumped in the back, a pounding thunder in his head.

Lincoln had two skilled running backs during Terrell's senior year. Still, when Terrell asked if he could carry the ball, head coach Vic Player did what he could. He made Terrell the team's fullback. Terrell blocked on most plays, but he did get to run with the ball enough to gain 700 yards and score three touchdowns. He even kicked off for the Hornets because he could kick farther than anyone else. Often he was the first player down the field to make the tackle.

"I wasn't like a superstar," Terrell said. "I was just another kid. I was just trying to get to college, really." Lincoln went 12–2 that year and played in the city championship game at Qualcomm Stadium. Terrell had no reason to think he would someday return to the field as a Super Bowl hero.

Eight players from Terrell's team got college Division 1-A scholarships. Terrell was one of them only because his brother Reggie played football at Long Beach State and convinced the coaches there to recruit him.

Long Beach State was not a football powerhouse.

Terrell during his senior year at Lincoln High

But the program was on the rise with coach George Allen, a former NFL head coach who had led the Washington Redskins to a Super Bowl. Terrell drove the two hours to Long Beach in an old Chevy Impala his mother had helped him buy. He moved into an apartment on campus and enrolled in classes. When Terrell joined his new teammates on the practice field, he and coach Allen quickly became friends.

Coach Allen saw Terrell's raw talent. He made Terrell the tailback on the **scout team,** meaning Terrell would be a **redshirt** freshman his first year while he learned how to run with the football.

Terrell's freshman year would officially begin the following season when he would take over as the team's starting tailback. That was the plan, anyway. Terrell was the star of the scout team, and coach Allen nicknamed him "Secretariat" after the great racehorse. The team finished 6–5, and the revival of the program drew national attention. But a few weeks after the season ended, coach Allen died of heart failure.

Long Beach State coach George Allen liked Terrell.

Former Oakland Raiders defensive back Willie Brown took over as coach. Terrell did not become the starting tailback as he had hoped. In 11 games as a backup, he scored two touchdowns and carried 55 times for 262 yards. The team won only two games, however, and attendance at games dropped. A week after the season ended, the football program was dropped. Suddenly, Terrell was without a team.

When Terrell's roommate told him that the recruiting coordinator from the University of Georgia had called, Terrell replied, "Where is Georgia?" He admitted later, "If you had given me a puzzle of the 50 states, I wouldn't have had any idea where to put Georgia." He visited Georgia anyway.

When Terrell arrived at the campus, he was impressed. The athletic hall was enormous, with trophies and championship banners everywhere. The football practice field was in better condition than the playing field back at Long Beach State. The locker room was huge, and a locker was already set up for Terrell with cleats and helmets and a jersey with his name on it. Terrell had two words for it all: "I'm here."

As a sophomore, Terrell played backup to Garrison Hearst, who would finish third in the Heisman

Trophy voting. Terrell rushed for 388 yards on just 53 carries for a dandy 7.3 yards-per-carry average and four scores that season.

The best thing that happened to Terrell that season was that his disability was diagnosed. One day during practice, as Terrell was suffering from another splitting headache, a team trainer said, "You ever heard of migraines, Terrell? You've got the classic symptoms." Trainers and doctors explained migraines to Terrell. "I tried to keep everything about my headaches to myself," he said. "I thought people would think I was crazy if I told them what it was like," he said. "Now I finally had a name for it. Some people said, 'Oh yeah, I get migraines too.' That gave me a sense of security. I figured if this many people have them, and they aren't dead, obviously these things aren't life-threatening."

Terrell appreciated the care packages of food and clothing that his mother often sent him. He studied hard to keep a B average in economics. He was eager for his junior season to start. With Garrison Hearst gone to the NFL, Terrell thought it was his time to shine. But head coach Ray Goff did not seem to like him. Coach Goff rarely spoke to Terrell and never praised him.

At one practice before the season started, Terrell injured his leg and collapsed to the ground in pain. His hamstring hurt so badly he could barely walk. Trainers took him to the locker room to give him treatment. Someone ran in and told Terrell that coach Goff wanted to see him right away. Terrell limped back out, and Goff yelled, "What are you doing? You're not hurt! Get back out there on the field!" Terrell started six games that season and gained 824 yards on 167 carries for a 4.9 average and five touchdowns. He also caught passes for three more scores.

Terrell hoped to make it to the NFL. He knew he would need a strong senior year to be drafted. During summer practice before the season, he still was not getting along with coach Goff. Terrell called Jamaul, who had just returned home from the Navy. Terrell asked Jamaul to come and live with him in Georgia. "Get out of that place, man, get out of San Diego," Terrell said. They could live together, just like old times. Jamaul loved the idea. A week later, Terrell's mother called. Jamaul had been shot dead. "I began thinking anything is possible in this world," Terrell said. "Anything. Good or bad. Anything."

Terrell struggled to fit in at Georgia.

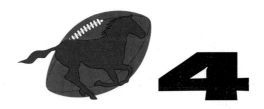

A Sudden Star

Terrell went to San Diego for Jamaul's funeral. While he was there, coach Goff called to tell him to hurry up and get back to Georgia. Terrell's senior season turned out worse than he expected.

Terrell suffered a slight hamstring injury in practice before the season opener, but coach Goff demanded that he play anyway. Playing made the injury worse. In the second game of the season, Terrell's hamstring popped. He had to miss the next three games. Coach Goff was so angry that he did not let Terrell stand on the sideline with his team. Coach Goff would not even give him a seat in the stands. Terrell had to buy a ticket and sit in the top row of the stadium just to see his team play. Terrell finished the season with just 445 yards rushing and seven touchdowns. "It was a sour situation," said Terrell. "The whole thing made me much tougher mentally. What doesn't kill you makes you stronger."

Terrell wondered if he would make it to the pros. At the annual NFL scouting camp, where hundreds of college athletes gather to try out for pro coaches and scouts, Terrell ran the 40-yard dash in 4.7 seconds. That is slow for a running back. "That's it," he said. "I'm camp meat." Terrell figured that, if he got picked at all, he would just be a human tackling dummy for the team that drafted him, and then he would be cut. But he did not give up.

Terrell knew the pro scouts would travel to all the college campuses to check out the players one last time before the spring draft. He had a month to prepare, and he was determined to be ready. He hired a personal trainer to put him through grueling sessions. When the scouts arrived a month later, Terrell impressed them with nifty moves and a fast 4.4-second 40. But was it enough?

Terrell, his mother, and his brothers gathered around the television for the April draft. They watched as the rounds went by. The Dallas Cowboys called during the fourth round. If Terrell didn't get drafted, would he be interested in coming to their camp as a **free agent?** Terrell's heart sank. A free agent? Rookie free agents rarely make a team.

Finally, in the sixth round, after 20 running backs had been chosen, the Denver Broncos took Terrell with the 196th pick. Denver? Terrell didn't even know the name of the Broncos coach. That night, Mike Shanahan called to introduce himself and congratulate Terrell.

Terrell figured his chance of making the Broncos was slim. Most professional teams keep just three tailbacks on their roster. The Broncos had six backs on their **depth chart,** in the following order:

1. Glyn Milburn
2. Rod Bernstine
3. Aaron Craver
4. Reggie Rivers
5. Sheldon Canley
6. Terrell Davis

Back when Terrell was growing up in San Diego, he had watched the Broncos quarterback John Elway routinely beat the local Chargers. In Denver's locker room the first day of camp, Terrell's knees buckled when he saw the great Elway in person.

And Elway was headed straight toward him! Terrell tried to play it cool as Elway extended his hand. "Nice to meet you," Terrell said. Elway grinned. "Nice to meet you, dude," he said. As soon as Elway was out of sight, Terrell ran to call his friends in Georgia and San Diego. "I just met John Elway!" he shouted.

In Denver's first preseason game, Terrell was sent in for one play. The coaches told him to carry the ball straight up the middle. He was stopped for no gain. The second game was against the Super Bowl champion San Francisco 49ers in Tokyo, Japan. The Broncos spent all week practicing in the sweltering Japanese heat. One of the team's practice rules was that when a running back got stopped, he had to sprint 40 yards more downfield and then run back to the huddle. By Thursday, Terrell had decided to quit. He tried to call the airlines to get on the next flight back to America, but the telephone operators spoke only Japanese. Terrell could not get through to the airlines. He would have to stay in Japan and fly back with the team after the game.

Terrell decided to make the best of it. Against the 49ers, the coaches let him carry the ball 11 times. He gained 46 yards and scored a touchdown. On the third-quarter kickoff, he delivered a bone-crunching hit on 49ers ball carrier Tyronne Drakeford. "He destroyed the guy, absolutely killed him," said tight end Shannon Sharpe. "When he did that, we all looked at each other and said, 'Man, we've got something special here.'" When Terrell reached his team's sideline, veteran tackle Michael Dean Perry told him, "On that hit alone, you just made the team." In the locker room after the game, coach Shanahan approached Terrell and said, "T. D., good job." Terrell thanked the coach and thought, *Cool, Coach knows who I am!*

Terrell moved up the depth chart to fifth string, to fourth string, to third string. He heard running backs coach Bobby Turner tell reporters, "You tell Terrell something once, he gets it. Tell him twice, he owns it. He's coachable." Four days before the regular-season opener, coach Shanahan sent for Terrell. Was he about to be cut, Terrell wondered. He entered the coach's office. Coach Shanahan was scribbling notes on a piece of paper. Terrell looked around the coach's office. Coach Shanahan finally looked up from his notes. "You know, T. D., you've been having a pretty good preseason," the coach said. "All the coaches like you. We're moving you up to the first team. You're our starting running back. Congratulations." Terrell tried to hide his smile, but he couldn't.

As a rookie in 1995, Terrell got off to a quick start.

Terrell signed a three-year contract for the rookie minimum of $166,000 a year. To celebrate, he bought a Ford Bronco and some furniture for his apartment in Denver. His wardrobe remained blue jeans and sweatpants, T-shirts, and frayed boxer shorts.

In the 1995 season opener at Mile High Stadium against the Buffalo Bills, Terrell rushed for 70 yards and a touchdown and the Broncos won, 22–7. In the second game, against the Dallas Cowboys at Texas Stadium, he carried for 61 yards in a 31–21 loss. In the third game, at home against the Washington Redskins, he rushed for 68 yards, caught seven passes for 61 more, and scored three touchdowns in a 38–31 victory.

Reporters asked Terrell to describe his running style. He said, "I run downhill." At home, Terrell would open the newspaper and see his name among the NFL rushing leaders—Barry Sanders, Emmitt Smith, Thurman Thomas, *Terrell Davis!*

He gained 97 yards against the New England Patriots and 135 against the Arizona Cardinals. "His work ethic is incredible," said coach Shanahan. When Terrell ran for 176 yards against San Diego, Shanahan said, "Everybody says to me, 'Oh, you're so smart for taking him in the sixth round.' Trust me, if we were so smart, we would have traded up for a first-rounder to get him. The thinking was that he could contribute on **special teams** as a rookie, then maybe play as time went on."

Even with their new star player, however, the Broncos weren't winners yet. They finished with an 8–8 record. Terrell's season ended when he tore a hamstring and missed the last two games. But by then, he had racked up 1,117 yards to become the lowest drafted player in NFL history to rush for more than 1,000 yards. "You could tell from the first day that Terrell was a different type of guy," said coach Shanahan. "He grew up the hard way. Everything he's gotten, he's earned the old-fashioned way."

By the 1996 season, everyone knew about Terrell's talent.

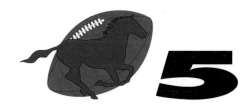

Rushing to Glory

The Broncos rewarded Terrell for his marvelous rookie year by tearing up the last two years of his original contract and giving him a new five-year, $6.8-million deal. Terrell rewarded the Broncos with six terrific games to start the 1996 season.

In the third game of the season, Terrell was on the field in the second quarter when bright lights flashed in his head. "I knew a migraine was coming, and I tried to stay in the game, but it wasn't possible," he said. "I sat down on the bench and told the trainers I had a migraine, and they gave me a nasal spray that numbs the migraine." Terrell returned in the second half to rush for 94 of his 137 yards and score the winning touchdown. Three games later, against the San Diego Chargers, he had another attack but again took the nasal spray and returned after 15 minutes to lead his team to victory.

The Broncos' offices were flooded with letters from people offering Terrell advice, much of it wacky. One person told Terrell to rub his head against the ground in a clockwise motion for 20 minutes. Another told him to drive to the top of a mountain and stand there for several hours. Yet another suggested putting tea bags on his eyes.

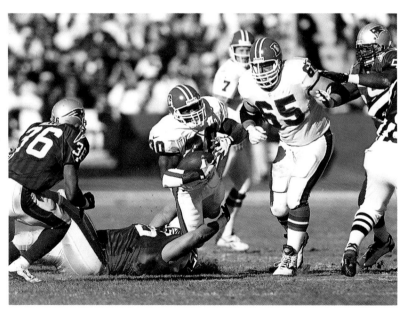

Terrell quickly became a key runner in Denver's offense.

Terrell thought the answer was more sleep. After his second attack, he turned his bedroom into a cave, installing tight window blinds and painting the walls black. And he took his anti-migraine pills. Terrell didn't have another migraine during a game until the 1998 Super Bowl.

During the 1996 regular season, Terrell led the Broncos to a 13—3 record and led the conference with 1,538 yards rushing. But the Jacksonville Jaguars upset Denver in the playoffs.

A month before the 1997 training camp, Terrell went to an orthodontist to get braces. Doctors had advised him that wearing braces might help to prevent migraines by stabilizing his jaw. "They make me look like a kid," Terrell said when he first saw them on his teeth. He found they made him even more popular with children. "Kids will say 'What's on your teeth, Terrell? Lemme see, lemme see!'" he said. "And I open my mouth wide, flash them a smile, let 'em see. After seeing them on an adult, they think braces are cool, and you know what? So do I."

Terrell rushed for more than 100 yards in each of the season's first three games, and the Broncos won all three. It was no secret that Terrell was the key to Denver's offense. "I've never had the responsibility of having to carry the offense, and that's something I welcome," he said. "I'm ready for the call." Whenever Terrell and his mates scored, they stood rigid and saluted each other. After a 38–20 victory over the Cincinnati Bengals, in which Terrell rushed for a team-record 215 yards, coach Shanahan handed him the game ball in the locker room and saluted him! The Mile High Salute had become the rage.

When Terrell rumbled for 171 yards against the New England Patriots in yet another Broncos win, Elway called him the best running back in the game and said, "He's what every quarterback wishes for."

"Hearing that from John means a lot," said Terrell. "John is cool." Terrell finished the year with 1,750 yards to lead the conference again even though he missed the last game with a separated shoulder.

His shoulder and ribs were still hurting a week later in a playoff game against the Jaguars, but he wasn't about to miss the game. He took a pain-killing injection in the locker room before the game and then powered for 184 yards and two touchdowns as the Broncos won, 42–17. A week later at noisy Arrowhead Stadium in Kansas City, he took another painkilling injection and pounded the Chiefs for 101 yards and both his team's scores in a 14–10 triumph.

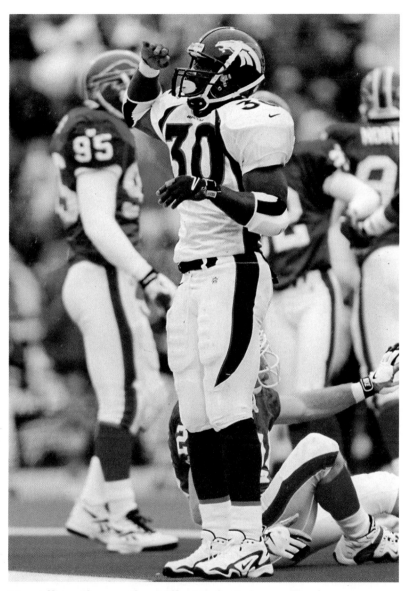

Terrell performs the Mile High Salute after a score.

The week after that, he had another shot before the AFC title game at Three Rivers Stadium in Pittsburgh and pummeled the Steelers for 139 yards in a 24–21 victory. His five touchdowns in three games showed that he isn't known as "T. D." just for his initials.

Three days before the Super Bowl, Terrell attended a ceremony at Lincoln High School where school officials retired his jersey number. Terrell's jersey was hung in Lincoln High School's glass trophy case, next to Marcus Allen's jersey.

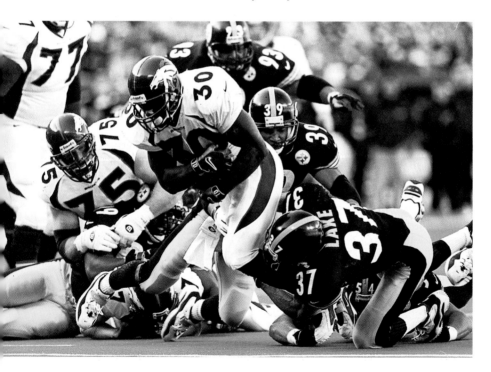

Terrell scored three touchdowns in the 1998 Super Bowl to beat the Green Bay Packers, 31—24. "I think the Packers have migraines at this point," said Terrell. After the team bus ride back to the hotel, Terrell went to his room where his mother, brothers, and friends were waiting. He celebrated with a chicken sandwich and french fries. By 11 P.M., everyone else left and Terrell went to bed.

The next day, he was whisked by limousine to downtown San Diego. NFL commissioner Paul Tagliabue presented him with the Super Bowl MVP trophy and a new Mustang convertible. Terrell gave the car to his brother Reggie, who drove it home to Latimer Street. The next day, nearly a million fans saluted and chanted "T. D! T. D! T. D!" as Terrell rode a fire truck through the streets of downtown Denver.

A week later, he started the Terrell Davis Migraine Foundation. "It's going to educate a lot of kids about what migraines really are," he explained. "There aren't going to be any seven-year-olds up all night crying and throwing up the way I was, having no idea what was wrong with them. Now they will know." He visited the White House and gave President Clinton a Broncos jersey and a Mile High Salute. "The dude even knew my name," said Terrell.

President Clinton receives a Broncos jersey from Terrell.

People saluted him at restaurants and malls and everywhere else he went. When he threw out the first pitch at the home opener for the San Diego Padres, batting champion Tony Gwynn asked him for his autograph. "I don't think I've completely mastered the idea of being famous yet," Terrell said.

The day before camp opened for the 1998–99 season, Terrell was sweeping his kitchen floor when the phone rang. It was coach Shanahan. "Hey," Terrell said, "what's up?" Terrell's salary was up. The Broncos had torn up his contract again and rewarded him, this time with a nine-year, $56.1 million contract, making him pro football's highest-paid running back. Terrell celebrated by buying himself a train set, some video games, and a remote-controlled car that he could buzz around in his backyard. For his mother, he bought a big house around the corner from him in Aurora, Colorado, so she could have plenty of room to raise her five young adopted children and grandchildren. Some of Terrell's brothers came to live in the house, too, and Terrell opened a construction company to provide them with jobs. He even began studying how to be a plumber, so he could work with his brothers in the off-season.

With the Broncos investing so much in him, Terrell figured he owed them his best effort. He arrived each morning for practice before anyone else so he could do individual drills, like bounding. Bounding is an exercise in which Terrell leaps with huge strides in slow motion up and down the field to develop his explosive legs. "I want to be able to run over defenders in the fourth quarter, when everybody on the field is tired," he said. "People look at me differently now. I can't go back now. If I go out there and have a bad season, I can't say, 'Well, you have to remember, I'm a sixth-round draft choice.' I can't use that anymore."

No one expected Terrell to do what he did in 1998 when he ran around, through, and over defenders for 2,008 yards—the third-highest total in NFL history. In just his fourth year, he had become nearly unstoppable, and fans across the Rocky Mountains were ready to celebrate another title. The Broncos were 13–0, three games from a perfect season, when the New York Giants beat them on a last-minute touchdown pass. Denver finished with a 14–2 record, beating the Seattle Seahawks in the finale as Terrell gained 178 yards to surpass the magical 2,000-yard mark. His record run came on "19 Handoff," a play that was about to propel the Broncos to the Super Bowl. When Terrell was told he had broken the 2,000-yard barrier, he said, "I don't care about yards. I don't care about stats. And I don't care about records. I care about winning."

The morning of the divisional playoff game against the Miami Dolphins, the NFL named Terrell its Most Valuable Player. Terrell smiled and said he was honored, but he had something else on his mind. The Dolphins had beaten the Broncos in the regular season. "That can't happen again," said Terrell. He made sure of that, ripping the Dolphins for 199 yards and two touchdowns as the Broncos won, 38—3. "You could see it in Terrell's eyes from the beginning," said Dolphins defender Sam Madison. "We let him have a chance to redeem himself, and that's what he did."

Spirits were sky-high a week later when Denver hosted the AFC Championship for the first time in nine years. The Broncos fell behind the New York Jets, 10—0, in the third quarter. Then Terrell took over. He led his team on a 20-point blitz in the third quarter, capped by his 31-yard scamper for a score on "19 Handoff." The Broncos won, 23—10, to earn their second straight trip to the Super Bowl.

Everyone expected the 1999 Super Bowl in Miami to be a running show. The Broncos, of course, had the best running back in football. And the NFC's Atlanta Falcons countered with tailback Jamal Anderson. For the first time in 50 years, the NFL's two leading rushers met in the title game. The Broncos won in a rout, 34—19, but not the way most people expected them to. Using Terrell as a distraction, Elway threw for 336 yards. "I don't mind being a decoy at all," Terrell said afterward. "We have a lot of key people on this team, and I'll do what I need to do to help us win championships."

But Terrell didn't just block all day. He rushed for

102 yards and caught two passes for 50 more. "I've never seen anybody break so many tackles," said Falcons coach Dan Reeves. Jamal Anderson was even more impressed. "It's scary," he said. "In terms of his cutting and vision, you see things that Terrell does now that he couldn't do two years ago. You wonder if we are ever going to be able to catch him."

The numbers say Terrell is the greatest running back in history. Terrell has run for more than 1,000 yards in each of his first three pro seasons and has won the conference rushing crown two times. His regular-season average of 105.1 yards a game is the highest ever, ahead of Jim Brown's 104.3 and Barry Sanders's 99.8. Terrell's playoff average of 142.5 yards blows away the next-highest average of 110, held by John Riggins.

But numbers don't say everything. Good deeds and modesty say more about someone than yardage totals. "I guess with success comes this superstar status that people like to hold you up to," Terrell says. "They make you feel like a superhero or something, but I like to tell them, 'Hey, I'm just like you.' I haven't discovered the cure for some deadly disease or anything, so I'm a little shocked when people react to me like I'm this amazing person. I'm just plain old Terrell."

Statistics

University of Georgia

Year	Games	Rushing Attempts	Yards	Avg	TDs	Receptions	Receiving Yards	TDs
1992	10	53	388	7.3	3	3	38	1
1993	11	167	824	4.9	5	12	161	3
1994	8	97	445	4.6	7	31	330	0
Totals	29	317	1,657	5.2	15	46	529	4

Denver Broncos

Year	Games	Rushing Attempts	Yards	Avg	TDs	Receptions	Receiving Yards	TDs
1995	14	237	1,117	4.7	7	49	367	1
1996	16	345	1,538	4.5	13	36	310	2
1997	15	369	1,750	4.7	15	42	287	0
1998	16	392	2,008	5.1	21	25	217	2
Totals	61	1,343	6,413	4.8	56	152	1,181	5

Career Honors

- Lowest draft choice in NFL history to rush for more than 1,000 yards in rookie year in 1995
- Football Digest NFL Rookie of the Year in 1995
- Led AFC in rushing in 1996
- Led AFC in rushing in 1997
- Led NFL in rushing in 1998
- Set NFL playoff scoring record with 8 touchdowns in 1998
- Super Bowl Most Valuable Player in 1998
- NFL Most Valuable Player in 1998

Glossary

cutback(s): A move in which the runner turns and runs at a sharp angle to the direction in which he or she was originally running.

depth chart: A list of the players who can play at each position. The best player is listed first.

down: A chance to advance the football. A team gets four downs to advance 10 yards or score.

free agent: A professional athlete who is free to play with any team because he or she does not have a contract.

handoff: The handing of the football to a teammate. The photo on the next page shows Denver quarterback John Elway giving Terrell the football on a handoff.

lupus: A disease in which chemicals in the person's body attack the body itself.

nose tackle: A defensive player who plays opposite the other team's center. Also called a *noseguard*.

quarterback sneak: A play in which the quarterback keeps the ball and runs straight forward.

Terrell takes a handoff from quarterback John Elway during the Broncos' Super Bowl victory over Atlanta in 1999. Elway retired after that game.

redshirt: A college athlete who does not compete for his or her team for a year so that he or she will be able to play another year.

scout team: Players who run the plays of their next opponent when practicing against their team's first string.

special teams: Players who play when their team is kicking off, trying for a field goal, or punting.

Sources

Information for this book was obtained from the following sources: Jim Armstrong (*Sport*, December 1998); Vickie Bane (*People*, 23 December 1996): Michael Bauman (*Milwaukee Journal Sentinel*, 26 January 1998); Terrell Davis (*TD: Dreams in Motion*, New York: HarperCollins, 1998) Denver Broncos media guide, 1998; Martin Dugard (*Esquire*, September 1998); Tom Friend (*ESPN, The Magazine*, 26 August 1998); Ron Kroichick (*San Francisco Chronicle*, 18 January 1999); Clay Latimer (*Football Digest*, February 1999); *Monday Night Football* (18 November 1998); Austin Murphy (*Sports Illustrated*, 28 October 1996); William Reed (*Sports Illustrated*, 1 November 1993); Adam Schefter (*Denver Post*, 3 February 1998, 10 January 1999, 18 January 1999); Patrick Saunders (*Denver Post*, 14 January 1999); Michael Silver (*Sports Illustrated*, 2 February 1998); Mark Starr (*Newsweek*, 11 January 1999).

Index

Write to Terrell:

You can send mail to Terrell at the address on the right. If you write a letter, don't get your hopes up too high. Terrell and other athletes get lots of letters every day, and they aren't always able to answer them all.

Terrell Davis
c/o Denver Broncos
13655 Broncos Parkway
Englewood, CO 80112

Acknowledgments

Photographs reproduced with permission of: Ryan McKee/© Rich Clarkson and Associates, p. 1; Eric Lars Bakke/© Rich Clarkson and Associates, pp. 9, 54, 62; © SportsChrome East/West/Rob Tringali Jr., pp. 2–3; © Andy Kuno/Endzone, pp. 6, 13; Courtesy of Kateree Davis, pp. 16, 19, 23, 24, 26, 27, 28; © Seth Poppel Yearbook Archives, p. 33; Courtesy of Long Beach State Sports Information Department, p. 34; © Courtesy of University of Georgia Athletic Association/Dale Zamine, p. 38; © ALLSPORT USA/Jamie Squire, p. 44; © SportsChrome East/West/Michael Zito, p. 46; © SportsChrome East/West/Vincent Manniello, p. 48; © ALLSPORT USA/Rick Stewart, p. 51; © ALLSPORT USA/Andy Lyons, p. 52; © SportsChrome East/West/Bryan Yablonsky, p. 61.

Front cover photograph by © ALLSPORT USA/Brian Bahr. Back cover photograph by *The Denver Post*.

Artwork by Michael Tacheny.

About the Author

Jeff Savage is a freelance writer and the author of more than 80 sports books for young readers. Among his other books for LernerSports are biographies of Eric Lindros, Mark McGwire, Tiger Woods and Julie Foudy. Jeff and his family live in Southern California.